"Jill Murphy deserves a constellation of gold stars for consistently writing picture books that please children and enrapture parents." *Observer*

When it was first published, the hilarious, loveable antics of the Large family in *Five Minutes' Peace* rang delightfully, wonderfully true – speaking to mums and little ones alike, and winning *Parents* magazine's Best Book for Babies Award. Thirty years on, this perennial family favourite – which has sold over one million copies worldwide – is as beautifully observed as ever, and has become an essential title for parents and children to share together.

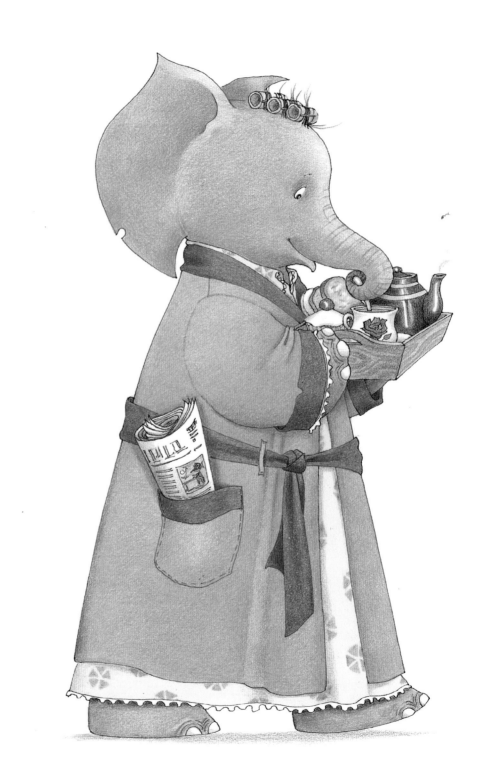

♬ ...with a little help from my friends. ♬

For Geoff, Sue, Abby, Hannah, Nick & Polly, with love.

First published 1986 by Walker Books Ltd
87 Vauxhall Walk, London SE11 5HJ

This edition published 2016

10 9

© 1986 Jill Murphy

The right of Jill Murphy to be identified as
author/illustrator of this work has been asserted by her
in accordance with the Copyright, Designs and Patents Act 1988

This book has been typeset in Bembo Educational

Printed in China

British Library Cataloguing in Publication Data:
a catalogue record for this book is available from the British Library

ISBN 978-1-4063-6190-2

www.walker.co.uk

Five Minutes' Peace

Celebrating Thirty Years of The Large Family

Jill Murphy

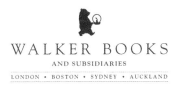

WALKER BOOKS

AND SUBSIDIARIES

LONDON · BOSTON · SYDNEY · AUCKLAND

The children were having breakfast.
This was not a pleasant sight.

Mrs Large took a tray from the cupboard.
She set it with a teapot, a milk jug, her
favourite cup and saucer, a plate of
marmalade toast and a leftover cake
from yesterday. She stuffed the morning
paper into her pocket and sneaked off
towards the door.

"Where are you going with that tray, Mum?" asked Laura.

"To the bathroom," said Mrs Large.

"Why?" asked the other two children.

"Because I want five minutes' peace from *you* lot," said Mrs Large.

"That's why."

"Can *we* come?" asked Lester as they trailed
     up the stairs behind her.

"No," said Mrs Large, "you can't."

"What shall *we* do then?" asked Laura.

"You can play," said Mrs Large. "Downstairs.
     By yourselves. And keep an eye on the baby."

"I'm *not* a baby," muttered the little one.

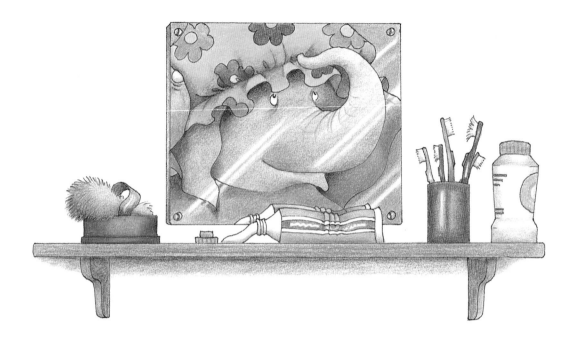

Mrs Large ran a deep, hot bath.

She emptied half a bottle of bath-foam into
the water, plonked on her bath-hat and got in.

She poured herself a cup of tea and lay back
with her eyes closed.

It was heaven.

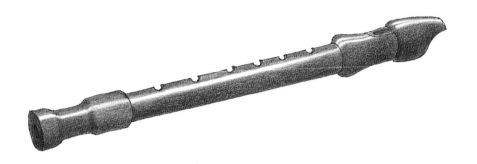

"Can I play you my tune?" asked Lester.

Mrs Large opened one eye. "Must you?" she asked.

"I've been practising," said Lester. "You told me to. *Can* I? Please, just for *one* minute."

"Go *on* then," sighed Mrs Large.

So Lester played. He played "Twinkle, Twinkle, Little Star" three and a half times.

In came Laura. "Can I read you a page from my reading book?" she asked.

"*No*, Laura," said Mrs Large. "Go on, *all* of you, off downstairs."

"You let Lester play his tune," said Laura.

"I heard. You like him better than me. It's not fair."

"Oh, don't be silly, Laura," said Mrs Large.

"Go *on* then. Just *one* page."

So Laura read. She read four and a half pages of "Little Red Riding Hood".

In came the little one with a trunkful of toys.
"For *you*!" he beamed, flinging them all
   into the bath water.
"Thank you, dear," said Mrs Large weakly.

"Can I see the cartoons in the paper?" asked Laura.

"Can I have the cake?" asked Lester.

"Can I get in with you?" asked the little one.

Mrs Large groaned.

In the end they *all* got in. The
little one was in such a hurry that
he forgot to take off his pyjamas.

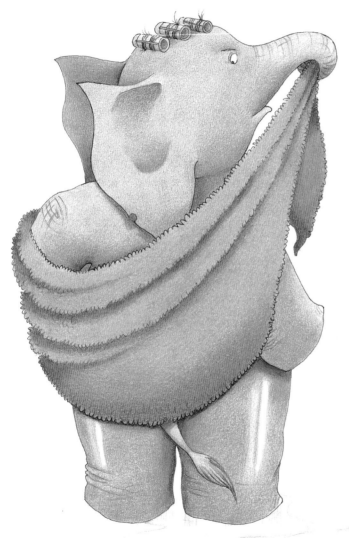

Mrs Large got out. She dried herself, put on her dressing-gown and headed for the door.

"Where are you going *now*, Mum?" asked Laura.

"To the kitchen," said Mrs Large.

"Why?" asked Lester.

"Because I want five minutes' peace from *you* lot," said Mrs Large.

"That's why."

And off she went downstairs,
where she had three minutes
and forty-five seconds of peace
before they all came to join her.

JILL MURPHY

is one of Britain's most treasured author–illustrators, who created her first book, the bestselling *The Worst Witch*, while still only eighteen. She is best known for her award-winning Large Family series – a series which has sold over five million copies worldwide, been adapted for television and includes the Kate Greenaway commended *All in One Piece* and the shortlisted *A Quiet Night In*. Among Jill's very popular characters is a small monster called Marlon, who appears in the acclaimed picture books *The Last Noo-Noo* and *All For One*. Jill lives in Cornwall.